Lester
Gets Lost

SIMON SMITH

Marshall Pickering

An Imprint of HarperCollins*Publishers*

BASED ON THE PARABLE OF THE LOST SHEEP, LUKE 15

Marshall Pickering is an Imprint of
HarperCollins*Religious*
part of HarperCollins*Publishers*
77-85 Fulham Palace Road, London W6 8JB
www.christian-publishing.com

First published in Great Britain in 2001 by Marshall Pickering

1 3 5 7 9 10 8 6 4 2

Simon Smith asserts the moral right to be
identified as the author and illustrator of this work.

A catalogue record for this book is
available from the British Library.

ISBN 0 551 03256 1

Printed in Hong Kong

For Shannon and Annalise

Down at the bottom
of a long-forgotten
garden four mice
were walking.

Fat Jim was taking his
friends to look at his pets.
His pets lived under
the woodpile.

Fat Jim had 43 pets.
Each one had a name.

There was…

Brynley   Jack   Kate

Jess   Sophie   Caleb   Zoe

Peter   Jimmy   Alfie   Hannah   Hattie

Loren   Grace   Rebekah   Joshua

Evie   James   Jonathan   Max   Eloise

Graham   Harry   Caroline   Tom

Paige   Mitch   Abi   Charis   Megan

Gary   Penny   Rachel   Laura

Jacob   Joel   Kerry   Robbie   Daniel

George   Polly   Sam   and   Lester.

Fat Jim took care of his pets.

He gave them clean water every day.

He fed them.

He cleaned them
up when they got
dirty.

He gave them
lots of exercise.

'Here are my pets,'
said Fat Jim.

'What are their names?'
said Big Al.

Fat Jim told Big Al
the names of his pets.

There was...

Brynley   Jack   Kate

Jess   Sophie   Caleb   Zoe

Peter   Jimmy   Alfie   Hannah   Hattie

Loren   Grace   Rebekah   Joshua

Evie   James   Jonathan   Max   Eloise

Graham   Harry   Caroline   Tom

Paige   Mitch   Abi   Charis   Megan

Gary   Penny   Rachel   Laura

Jacob   Joel   Kerry   Robbie   Daniel

George   Polly   and   Sam.

'Oh no!' said Fat Jim. 'Lester is not here.
He must have got lost.'

'Don't worry,' said Stumpy.

'I'm sure you won't miss him much,'
said Big Al.

'You've still got lots of other pets left here
to look after,' said Bodge.

'I have to find Lester,' said Fat Jim.
'We'll help you,' said Stumpy.

And the mice
set off to look
for Lester.

Stumpy looked
under the shed.

He looked behind
the water barrel.

He looked into all
of the plant pots.

He searched through
the weedy patch.

He looked around the compost heap.
He didn't find Lester, but he did find
a shiny conker.

Big Al looked under
the scruffy hedge.

He looked behind
the gate.

He looked into
the pond.

He searched through
the long grass.

He looked around the brick pile.
He didn't find Lester, but he did
find an old metal spoon.

Bodge looked under
the rusty spade.

He looked behind
the wooden fence.

He looked into
the old bucket.

He searched through
the pile of leaves.

He looked round the concrete gnome.
He didn't find Lester, but he did find
a long-lost toy soldier.

The mice were very tired. They had been looking for Lester all afternoon.

Stumpy, Big Al and Bodge went home to sleep.

But Fat Jim went on
searching for Lester.

He looked all
over the place.

It was getting dark.
But Fat Jim kept
on looking.

He looked under the
roots of the old tree.

He looked behind
the rocky mound.

He looked into
the broken pipe.

He searched through
the leafy bushes.

He looked around
the toadstools
and the anthills.

He even looked in
the muddy puddles.

Suddenly, Fat Jim
heard a noise.

He lifted up an old
watering can and
there was…

…Lester!

Fat Jim picked Lester up and rushed home with him.

Stumpy, Big Al and Bodge were very excited to see them.

Fat Jim's pets were excited too.

'You are very special, Lester,' said Fat Jim,
'because you got lost, but now
I've found you.
It's good to
have you
home again.'